For Luke

Copyright © Peter Kavanagh 1993

First published in 1993
by Simon and Schuster Young Books

Reprinted in 1997
by Macdonald Young Books
61 Western Road
Hove
East Sussex
BN3 1JD

Laserset in 18pt Veljovic by Alphabet Typesetting (London) Limited
Printed and bound in Belgium by Proost N.V.

British Library Cataloguing in Publication Data available

ISBN 0 7500 1373 7
ISBN 0 7500 1374 5 (pbk)

THERE'S A MONSTER NEXT DOOR!

Peter Kavanagh

MACDONALD YOUNG BOOKS

Robby Brown had a problem. He lived next door to a monster.

He was not exactly sure what kind of monster it was.

He knew it had huge, hairy hands because once
he saw it bringing in a parcel.

And he knew that it liked to roar about at night because sometimes he heard it. RRAAAAAARRRGGH!

On Mondays, when Mum put the bin bag out, there was always a huge pile of rubbish outside the monster's house.

But Robby's mum and dad did not believe there was
a monster next door.

Robby decided he would have to do something about the monster.
He couldn't go on living beside it, waiting for it to come and get him.

He would take a photo of it. Then Mum and Dad would believe
him and Mum would send Dad round to make the monster go away.

The next day, shaking all over, Robby went round
to the monster's house.

When he got there, he was too scared to knock.
But suddenly the door opened...

There stood the monster!
Robby Brown fainted.

When he woke up he was lying on a monster
sofa with a bag of ice on his head.

The monster came in with some milk and biscuits.
"You gave me quite a fright," it said. "I'm not used to visitors."

"Would you like to play some games?" asked the monster.

That afternoon the monster showed Robby how to play chase. CRASH! BANG! CRASH!

And how to roar. RRAAAAAARRRGGH!

And how to throw things about. *Wheeeeeee* CRASH!

When it was tea-time, Robby went back to his own house.
He had forgotten about taking a photo.

During tea he practised throwing things about.
Wheeeeeee CRASH!

Then he chased teddy around until it was time for bed.
CRASH! BANG! CRASH!

And he roared at Mum when she took him up for a bath.
RRAAAAAARRRGGH!

"We've got a problem," said Dad.
"That boy is turning into a right monster!"

"RRR!" said Robby.